This book is a work of fiction. Any references to historical events, real people, or real places are used fictitiously. Other names, characters, places, and events are products of the author's imagination, and any resemblance to actual events or places or persons, living or dead, is entirely coincidental.

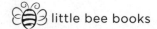 little bee books

An imprint of Bonnier Publishing USA
251 Park Avenue South, New York, NY 10010
Copyright © 2017 by Bonnier Publishing USA
All rights reserved, including the right of reproduction in whole or in part in any form. LITTLE BEE BOOKS is a trademark of Bonnier Publishing USA, and associated colophon is a trademark of Bonnier Publishing USA.

Library of Congress Cataloging-in-Publication Data:
Names: Kent, Jaden, author. | Bodnaruk, Iryna, illustrator.
Title: The cave of Aaaaah! doom! / by Jaden Kent; illustrated by Iryna Bodnaruk.
Description: First edition. | New York: Little Bee Books, [2017] | Series: Ella and Owen; #1 | Summary: A young dragon named Ella convinces her twin brother Owen to join her on a bold quest to find a wizard that will help cure Owen of his flaming cold. | Identifiers: LCCN 2016003000 | Subjects: | CYAC: Brothers and sisters—Fiction. | Twins—Fiction. | Adventure and adventurers—Fiction. | Dragons—Fiction. | Ghouls and ogres—Fiction. | Wizards—Fiction. | Magic—Fiction. | Humorous stories. Classification: LCC PZ7.1.K509 Cav 2017 | DDC [Fic]—dc23 | LC record available at https://lccn.loc.gov/2016003000

Printed in the United States of America LB 0217
First Edition 2 4 6 8 10 9 7 6 5 3 1
ISBN 978-1-4998-0393-8 (hc)
ISBN 978-1-4998-0368-6 (pb)
littlebeebooks.com
bonnierpublishingusa.com

ELLA AND OWEN

THE CAVE OF AAAAAH! DOOM!

by
Jaden Kent

little bee books

illustrated by
Iryna Bodnaruk

TABLE OF CONTENTS

1
WHEN DRAGONS SNEEZE

On the other side of Fright Mountain, through the Fog of Screams and past the Waterfall of Destruction, was a place where only knights in shining armor dared to go when they wanted to impress a princess.

At the bottom of the other side of the mountain was Dragon Patch. Dozens of dragons lived there in dozens of stone houses.

That's right.

Dragons!

Do you know all there is to know about dragons? Here are a few important things:

They have really stinky breath—actually, really stinky *fire* breath.

You can ride them like a flying horse!

They have wings.

And claws.

And their favorite dessert
is pickled-fish Popsicles!
Is there more?
You bet! They
sometimes get sick. And
when fire-breathing
dragons sneeze, you
had better run for cover. . . .

"AH-CHOO!"

A ball of fire shot from Owen's mouth. It shot across his bedroom, out the window, and then lit on fire a toadstool that his twin sister, Ella, was sitting on.

"Blazing scales! You made me drop my spider snail!" Ella said as her eight-legged pet slimed away. Very slowly.

"Sorry," Owen said.

"You've been sick since forever," Ella said. "At least five whole days. And fire sneezes are *not* normal."

"But I'm okay being sick," Owen said.

Owen may have been okay being sick, but there was a long list of things Owen *wasn't* okay with. The top three were:

1.
Evil Wizards

SCARY!

2.
Vegetables

YUCK!

3.
Evil Wizards
Made of
Vegetables

THE WORST!

Owen was very okay having a cold because it meant he could stay in bed and read. All day. Owen *loved* to read about hairy trolls, magical fairies, and heroic dragons. He especially loved books about dragons who defeated knights in shining armor.

"Mom says if I keep the slugs out of my ears and eat my slime, I'll be flying around in no time," Owen explained as he lifted a large rock and slurped the green gunk on the bottom. Owen's nose wiggled. He was going to sneeze again. *"Ah . . . ah . . . ah . . ."*

Ella flew into Owen's bedroom cave and grabbed a bucket of cold swamp water that was sitting by his bed. She threw it into his open mouth before he could sneeze flames. Steam puffed from his ears.

"There! That should do it!" Ella said.

Owen quickly shook his head. *"AH-CHOO!"* he sneezed.

A spray of water shot from his mouth and soaked Ella.

"Yuck! Sick brother!" Ella shook like a wet pixie at Lava Lake.

"Mom says I'll be fine in, like, a day or two . . . or ten." Owen turned away from his sister, cracked open a very good book about a dragon who defeated an evil wizard made of vegetables, and began to read.

"*I* don't want you to be sick anymore," Ella said.

"Aww . . . thanks for caring, Sis!" Owen said.

"Well, it's kinda mostly because I know Mom will make me do your chores if you're sick," Ella admitted.

Owen looked straight ahead and ignored his sister.

She tried to get his attention again. "So, I've heard of a cave where a mystical wizard dragon has a secret cure for everything. He once changed a frog into a toad. He even turned a potato into something called a French fry—or so I'm told."

"Sorry, I don't want to go," Owen said and went back to reading his book.

"But it'll be an awesome adventure!" Ella said.

"Now for *sure* I don't want to go," he said.

"And exciting!" Ella added.

"I double even *more* don't want to go."
He turned a page in his book. The evil
wizard made of vegetables had just cast a
broccoli spell.

"*And* we can collect
ogre toenails for your
ogre toenail collection,"
Ella said and sighed.

"Ogre toenails?"
Owen closed his book
and sat up in his bed.
"Oooh! *Now* I want to go!"

The excitement of the
toenails made his nose twitch.
Then twitch again. Then *"AH-CHOO!"*
Fire shot from his nose, and the force
of the sneeze threw him across the room.
He bounced off the wall and tumbled
across the cave.

Owen rubbed his nose with his tail. "Just one question. What's the name of this dragon wizard guy?"

"Dragon Wizard Orlock Morlock. He lives in a cave," Ella said.

"Does the cave have a name?" Owen asked.

"Nope," she said.

"Not possible," Owen replied. "All caves have names, according to the Cave Naming Rules of Sir Stonecastle Rockhound. Like, there's the Cave of Evil Bunny Rabbits, the Cave of Evil Fairies, the Cave of Evil Unicorns. . . ."

"Those creatures don't sound very friendly," Ella said.

"Uh, *yeah*. Why do you think they live in *caves*?" Owen answered.

"Well, this place is just called the, uh, Cave of, uh, Caves," Ella explained. "Because it's a cave full of caves. That aren't evil."

"I don't know." Owen began to have second thoughts. "It sounds kinda iffy. . . ."

"Ogre toenails!" Ella reminded him with a hopeful smile.

Owen got excited again. "What are we waiting for? Let's go!"

The two rushed from their cave, wings flapping.

Ella didn't tell Owen that she made up the name the Cave of Caves. She also didn't tell him the cave was *really* called the Cave of Aaaaah! Doom!

But don't worry. Owen figured that one out soon enough.

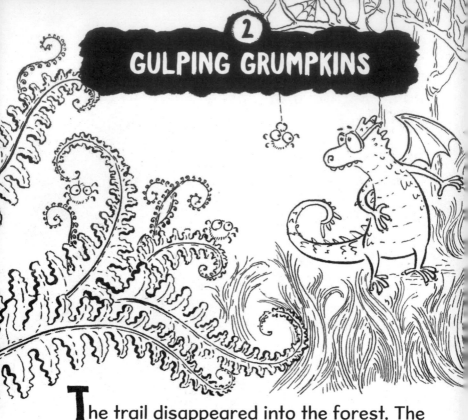

The trail disappeared into the forest. The dirt path was long gone, covered in weeds. As they walked, the twins heard an animal howl nearby.

"We're lost, aren't we?" Owen asked.

"I did *not* get us lost!" Ella said defensively.

"This is what I get for following you,"
Owen huffed.

"I'll have you know that I'm using my . . .
uh . . . using my cave-finding dragon skills
to find the Cave of Caves!" Ella exclaimed.

"Dragons don't have cave-finding skills,"
Owen said. "You're making that up."

"Quiet please. I will first use my sense of dragon smell to find the trail. . . ."

"We don't have dragon smell," Owen said.

"*Shhh* . . . the cave is this way," she said as she pointed straight ahead.

Thinking quickly, Ella picked up a rock and held it to one ear. "Now I will hold up this rock and listen to what it says. . . ." she said.

"I think that's only for seashells down at Firebreather Beach," Owen said.

"Shhh," she shushed. "It's telling me the way." Ella pointed forward. "There!" she said.

"You expect me to believe that?" Owen asked.

"The rock speaks the truth," Ella said.

Owen reluctantly followed Ella deeper into the forest. They went past the dragonberry bushes, over Unicorn Bridge, and down into the Forest of Shadows, until the trees blocked out the sun.

Owen looked around. "I think your rock got us more lost than you did."

Ella shook the rock. "It must've lost its power in the forest," she said nervously.

"Great. Now we're even more lost," Owen said, "because of a rock."

"*Shhh* . . . I'm thinking," she said.

Instead of being quiet, Owen shouted, "Ella! Look over there!"

Owen took off, wings flapping. "It's a tree sprite! Being lost just got so much better!"

Fluttering between the branches of an old willow tree was something truly rare. It was a tiny rainbow-colored creature flapping its wings as it moved under the leaves.

"Tree sprite? Really?" said Ella. "Looks more like a water sprite to me."

"It wants to play!" Owen said as he chased the sprite.

The sprite peeked out from around a leaf and then zoomed off.

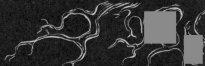

Owen was about to chase it again, but he realized just in time that he was at the edge of a steep hill. "Whoa! That was close," he said as his claws grasped the edge of the hill. He waved good-bye as the sprite flew away.

Ella ran to catch up, but she crashed into Owen. Together, they fell over the edge.

"We're—" said Owen.

BOUNCE!

"Falling—" said Ella.

BOING!

"Down—" said Owen.

BOING!

"The hill!" said Ella.

BOUNCE!

"OOOMPH!" They tumbled to the bottom and landed in a prickle patch filled with vines. On the vines were bright-green melons that looked like big monster heads.

"Grumpkins!" cried Owen.

"Ooh!" Ella said. "I hear they're delicious!"

"I'm not eating anything that looks like it has a face," said Owen, "even if it *is* a fruit."

"Suit yourself." Ella popped a grumpkin into her mouth and spit the seeds onto the ground. "That's so good it makes my scales shiver."

"Umm . . . I wouldn't eat any more of those," Owen said. He pointed to a sign that said: NO EATING! EXCEPT ME EATING YOU!

Ella ignored her brother's warning. She grabbed another plump grumpkin.

Owen snatched it from her. "Not a good idea," he said.

"But a tasty one," she said.

"But the sign!" Owen said nervously.

The sign reads: "No EATING! EXCEPT ME EATING YOU!"

"Signs aren't as yummy." Ella swung her tail around like a whip. She poked the pointy end into the grumpkin and pulled it from Owen.

The long vine attached to the grumpkin pulled back tightly. Ella pulled harder. "It's stuck on something," she said.

Owen followed the vine. It wrapped around a tree branch over their heads. At the end of the vine was a large wooden cage. "Uh, Ella, you should really let go. . . ." he said.

NO EATING! EXCEPT ME EATING YOU!

SNAP!

The vine broke in half.

A cage released and dropped over the two dragons.

"Now you've done it!" Owen squealed. "You got us lost, and now we're trapped—trapped like, well, dragons in a cage in the middle of nowhere."

"You wanted adventure and excitement, right?" Ella said. "This is it!"

"I didn't want either of those things!" Owen grabbed the cage and shook it. "I don't suppose you have any dragon sense for cage-breaking?" Owen asked.

The bushes rustled. The sound of two stomping feet came toward them. A large green creature stepped into the clearing. Flies swarmed around his head. His wart-covered legs poked from his purple shorts. When he spoke, a cloud of belly moths shot past his yellow teeth and filled the air.

"Caught two dragons for lunch! That is what I have done," the ogre said.

"You're serving lunch?" Ella asked.

"I don't think we're his guests," Owen said. "I think *we're* his lunch. . . ."

THE OGRE'S FEAST

"**B**ut you can't eat us!" Owen cried out.

"Our scales are tough like tree bark," Ella said. "Our stomachs are full of beetle skeletons, and we taste terrible!" Ella turned and licked her brother. "Blegh! See?! He tastes awful!" she said.

"Sorry, I've been sick," Owen said. "My nose is full of dragon boogers and fire."

Ella and Owen sat in their cage on the floor of the ogre's messy hut. The barefoot ogre stomped over to them. "Osgood Ogresteen. That is who I am," he said. "Of the ogres in Ogreville, I am the mean one. Eating dragons, that's what I do."

Owen looked around the hut. There was
a huge cooking pot of bubbling brown
goo over a fire. Jars of spices hung from
hooks on the ceiling. A stack of old bones
was piled against the back wall.

Osgood put on a large chef's hat. He
tilted it to the right and then to the left.
"You are in big trouble for eating my
grumpkins is what you is," he said. "Gimme
back the grumpkin you did eat, or into my
stew pot goes you."

Ella's eyes widened in shock. "I can't replace the grumpkin. I ate it."

"Suit yourself," said Osgood. "Grumpkin stew, dragon stew—no difference is there to my belly."

"My sister is sooooo, so sorry, Mr. Osgood, sir," Owen said. "She won't do it again."

Osgood plopped spices into his bubbling cauldron. "A sniffle of bat curry, claws dried from a newt, three drops of owl's hoot, two rattles of a snake, and a leg of spider. Oh, and let's not forget fiery lava salt and a splash of scarlet red pepper."

Ella perked up at the mention of the pepper. "Pepper? Did you say pepper?"

"Pepper is fav-fav-favorite for me," the ogre said.

Ella smiled. "Wellll, if you're going to make a cauldron of dragon stew, I know a very secret dragon secret that'll make it the best dragon stew in Ogreburg."

"No!" the ogre said. "Ogreville is where Osgood lives."

"Right! And you could be the king of Ogre-wherever with my cooking secret," Ella replied.

"Tell me this secret stew knowledge!" Osgood said.

"Promise to keep it a secret?" Ella asked.

"All secrets are kept secret with me!" Osgood replied.

"Very well," Ella said. "If you want the yum-yum-yummiest dragon stew, the best thing to do is put a little pepper on the dragon before you cook him."

Osgood grabbed a few pinches of pepper and threw them at Ella.

Ella sneezed. "Don't forget the other dragon. Two's better than one."

Owen backed up in the cage. "Oh no. I'm not a fan of pepper. Really."

"But I am so much a fan of making you yummy to my tummy." Osgood threw a big handful of pepper at Owen. It landed right on Owen's nose.

Owen's nose twitched. His nostrils wiggled. His scales shook and rattled. His tail whipped in a circle. "Woo-woo-woo!" he yelled. He tilted his head back and his whole body shook as he sneezed a blaze of dragon fire. *"AH-CHOO!"* Fire shot out of his mouth and scorched the cage.

Osgood stumbled backward. *"Aaaaah! Dragon fire!"* he shouted.

"AH-CHOO!" More fire shot out.

"AH-CHOO!" Then even more fire!

"Got to get away from the dragon fire!" Osgood screamed as he opened up a wooden trunk and jumped in, slamming the lid closed.

Ella pushed against the door of their cage. It swung wide open. "My plan worked beautifully!" she said.

"That was a plan?" Owen asked.

"Yup. Now just run and don't stop!" Ella ran for the door of the hut, but Owen stayed put and looked around.

"Hang on!" he said. Owen ran to the ogre's spice shelves and grabbed a jar of ogre toenail clippings.

He paused to think for a second, and then he looked down, popped dragon lint from his belly button, and placed it on the shelf where the jar was. "Good trade!" Owen said. "Thanks, Osgood!"

"Thanks to you for not sneezing fire on me again, oh mighty dragon!" Osgood called out from inside the trunk.

"Who knew ogres were so afraid of fire?" Owen yelled to his sister.

"**R**un!" Ella yelled.

"No way!" Owen replied. "We've got wings! Let's go!"

Ella and Owen flew out of Osgood's hut
as quickly as they could.

"Thank you for eating me not!" was the
last they heard from the ogre.

When they were safely away, Ella smiled. "Say it," Ella said.

"Nope," Owen replied.

"Come on. Say it," Ella said again.

"Nope," said Owen.

"Just once! You know I earned it!" Ella said.

"Okay! Okay! *Fine!* Thanks for saving my scales, Ella," Owen said. "I did *not* want to end up as dragon stew!"

"Don't worry, bro! There's no way I'm letting anything eat you!" Ella replied. "Mom and Dad would ground me for one thousand years if I did."

With Ella leading the way, the two dragons soon arrived at a dark and creepy cave. A chill shot through Owen's wings as they landed at the vine-covered entrance.

"I told you we'd find it!" Ella cheered.

"Who . . . who told you about this place?" Owen asked nervously.

"A tree elf named Branchy McElffenberry," Ella replied.

Owen peered into the cave. "This place is blacker than Mom's toadstool pie. Are you *sure* this is the Cave of Caves?"

"Sure, I'm sure that I'm sure!" Ella said quickly.

"If this *is* the Cave of Caves, then why does the sign say the Cave of Aaaaah! Doom!?" Owen asked, pointing to an old, broken sign that said the CAVE OF AAAAAH! DOOM! in big red letters underneath a screaming skeleton head.

"Because dragon wizards can't spell!"
Ella offered. "Let's get flapping, bro!"

"Swear on your horns that you're telling
the truth!" Owen said as he glared at Ella
with his yellow eyes.

"Okay, so maybe I sort of, just a teeny
tiny little bit, kinda, but not much, didn't
tell you the *whole* truth about the cave's
name," Ella admitted. "But Branchy
McElffenberry said this *is* where the
Dragon Wizard Orlock Morlock lives!"

"Aw, dragon scales! I almost got turned
into stew for *this*?!" Owen huffed. "I'm
going home!"

"AH-CHOO!" A fire sneeze shot from Owen's mouth and sent him flying out of control.

PING!

ZING!

ZOOM!

Owen bounced about like a rubber dragon egg until he smacked into the sign that said the CAVE OF AAAAAH! DOOM! The skeleton head fell off above the sign and bonked him on the head.

"On second thought, lead the way," Owen said as he rubbed his aching head. "I've gotta get rid of this cold."

Owen hid behind Ella as the two dragons tiptoed on their pointy claws and carefully crept into the dark cave.

"Hey, why can't wizards ever live in a place called the Cave of Yay! Fun and Happiness!?" Owen whispered.

"Because that's where all the *fairies* live," Ella whispered back. "And fairies don't like wizards because they steal all their magic fairy flour to make Wicked Wizard Waffles."

The siblings stopped in their tracks as they heard a loud *GROWL!*

"Please tell me that was your tummy rumbling," Ella said.

"No, it wasn't me, because my tummy doesn't have *big, scary eyes!*" Owen shouted and pointed to two huge eyes glowing in the darkness.

Their eyes blinked, and then the siblings heard a cave-rumbling *ROAR!*

Ella and Owen were frozen in fear. They heard another *ROAR!* that echoed through the cave. Something big and square swooped down on them from above. It had brown wings; sharp, stabby fangs; red eyes; and smelled like breakfast.

"*AAAAAH!* It's a giant Wicked Wizard Waffle!" Ella screamed.

"*DOOOOOM!*" Owen yelled. He paused for a moment and then said proudly, "Hey! Now we know why they call this place the Cave of Aaaaah! Doom!"

Ella and Owen gave each other a quick glance, and then both yelled, "RUN!"

The panicked dragons flapped their wings to escape. Instead of exiting quickly, they bonked into each other and fell to the ground.

"What do Wicked Wizard Waffles hate?!" Ella asked as the monster waffle swooped toward them.

"Very small puppies?!" Owen asked.

"No!"

"Gnomes!" Owen guessed.

"No!"

"Well they *should* hate gnomes. They're annoying!" Owen said.

"They don't hate gnomes!" Ella replied. "They hate music, so start singing!"

"Pixie bells, ogres smell, vampires hate the day! When a dragon flies and blows its fire, the villagers run away!" Ella and Owen sang as loud as they could.

The Wicked Wizard Waffle covered its
buttery ears and flew from the cave to
escape their horrible singing. The siblings
turned and gave each other a high five.

"I've never been so happy that you sing so terribly!" Ella said, relieved.

But Ella and Owen weren't out of trouble yet!

"Don't move!" someone called out from behind them.

Ella and Owen spun around and came face-to-face with a wizard! It had:

CELERY ARMS!

CARROT LEGS!

A BROCCOLI BODY!

A CAULIFLOWER HEAD!

A POINTY HAT!

It wasn't *just* a wizard! It was an . . .

"EVIL VEGETABLE WIZARD!" Owen screamed. *"AAAAAH! DOOOOOM! AGAIN!"*

"Why did you sing to my Wicked Wizard Waffle?!" the evil vegetable wizard yelled. He pointed his asparagus wand at them. "Tell me why you're here, or I'll use my magic to make a really grumpy pancake!"

"I think he's serious!" Ella said.

"Of *course* he's serious!" Owen replied. "He's a vegetable!"

"We don't want any trouble," Ella explained. "We're looking for the Dragon Wizard Orlock Morlock."

"*I* am the wizard Orlock Morlock!" The vegetable wizard waved his wand in the air to look dramatic.

Owen glared at Ella. "I thought Stumpy McElf-face or whatever his name is said Orlock Morlock was a *dragon* wizard?!"

Ella shrugged her shoulders. "That's the last time I trust a tree elf," she said.

The two dragons were in a cage. *Again.*

Orlock pushed the door closed.

SLAM!

"I'm tired of everyone putting us into a cage!" Ella complained.

The vegetable wizard had taken the two dragons to his wizard dungeon deep in the cave. Torches lit the room. Next to Orlock's workbench was a large statue of a winged lion. On top of the statue was a clear crystal ball. Dozens of magic items hung from the walls, which were covered in slimy moss and smelled like an old shoe.

"What're you going to do with us?" Ella asked.

"Turn you into flying monkeys!" Orlock answered as he rubbed his parsley beard.

"That's not a very nice thing to do!" Ella said.

"They don't call us evil wizards because we do *nice* things!" Orlock sneered.

"Can my wings have racing stripes?" Owen asked.

Ella glared at Owen. "You're not helping!"

"What? At least he's not going to turn us into flying bunny rabbits," Owen said.

Orlock perked up. "Great idea! Flying bunnies are even funnier than flying monkeys!"

"I know how you can make sure we have *huge* bunny ears!" Ella said, thinking quickly.

"If it needs magic fairy flour, don't bother. I used all of mine to make that giant waffle you two chased away," Orlock said.

"Nope. All you need to do is pour some pepper on Owen," Ella explained. "It'll make him grow huge bunny ears bigger than a unicorn's horn."

"Nice try! If I dump pepper on him, he'll sneeze fire, I'd bet. Do you think I'm as dumb as an ogre or something?" Orlock raised his asparagus wand to turn them into flying bunnies.

"Wait!" Owen yelled. "Maybe there's something we could trade you so you'll set us free?"

Orlock thought for a moment, the asparagus wand still held over his head. "Well, there *is* one thing I'd be willing to trade."

"Name it!" Owen said.

"Dragon belly button lint for my lint collection!" Orlock said.

Owen smiled a big smile. "I've got plenty right—"

He looked down at his belly button and his smile faded. He had left all his belly button lint with Osgood the ogre. Owen looked to Ella (who washes her belly button every morning) and sighed. "I hope you like being a flying bunny rabbit."

Owen and Ella hugged each other.

Orlock waved his wand and . . . *POOF!*
The two dragons grew long bunny ears.

"Uh, we're still more dragon than bunny rabbit," Ella said as she wiggled her fuzzy ears.

Orlock waved his asparagus wand again.

POOF!

Now Ella and Owen had fuzzy bunny tails.

"Nope. Still not bunnies," Owen said.

A frustrated Orlock waved his wand again and again and again.

With each wand wave, Orlock turned Owen and Ella into dragons with bunny teeth, dragons with cute pink noses, and dragons with big white bunny feet. But the one thing Orlock could *not* turn them into was plain old bunny rabbits with wings.

"Are you *sure* you're an evil wizard?" Owen asked.

"Yes! But . . . I'm just terrible at casting spells! All I can do is turn broccoli into cauliflower!" Orlock threw his wand to the ground and started to cry.

Ella and Owen couldn't help but feel sorry for him.

"Don't cry, Orlock. It'll just make you soggy," Ella said.

"Maybe there's some way we can help?" Owen said.

Orlock wiped his tears and picked up his floppy asparagus wand. "It'd help if you could turn my asparagus wand into a rhubarb wand. Those are *really* powerful!"

"Um, not really sure how we'd do that . . ." Ella looked to Owen, who shrugged.

"We'd need ogre toenails to make the magic potion, but the ogre down the trail always tries to make stew out of me when I go to ask for some," Orlock explained.

"*We* have ogre toenails!" Ella flapped her wings in excitement.

"No way!" Owen hugged the ogre toenails against his chest. "I traded my best belly button lint for these!"

"Give him the toenails!" Ella tried to grab the jar away. "If you do, you can have my dessert for a week!"

"Chocolate-covered caterpillars?" Owen asked.

"Yes!" Ella said and tugged the jar.

"Make it three weeks!" Owen said and tugged it back.

"Two weeks!"

"Deal!"

Owen yanked the jar of ogre toenails from Ella and gave it to Orlock.

"Let's make a rhubarb wand!" Owen said.

8
ORLOCK THE NOT-SO-EVIL WIZARD

Orlock proudly waved his new rhubarb wand in the air!

"It worked! It worked! It worked!" Orlock sang and danced. "I turned my asparagus wand into a rhubarb wand!"

"Remember our deal! We gave you the ogre toenails. You have to let us go! And cure me!" Owen said.

"*And* you have to also stop being evil," Ella added.

Orlock stopped dancing. "Can I still be evil on weekends?" he asked hopefully. "Pleeease?"

"Mondays only," Ella said. "Because everybody already hates Mondays."

"And holidays? You can't expect me to *not* be evil on Evil-mas—" Orlock said.

"Great! Evil on Evil-mas," Owen cut in. "Now please cure me before I—*AH-CHOO!*"

Too late!

BING!

BANG!

BONK!

Fire shot from Owen's mouth like a rocket ship blasting off. He bounced around the dungeon like a soccer ball being kicked by ten trolls, before rolling to a stop in front of a jar filled with bat wings.

"You kept up your end of the deal, and now it's time for me to do my part." Orlock pointed his rhubarb wand at Owen. "Oh, and if this turns you into a Prickle Pie Toad, I'm sorry. I'm just not very good with spells."

"Wait!" Owen shouted.

But it was too late! Again!

SHOOM!

A magic glimmer shot from Orlock's rhubarb wand and surrounded Owen. Owen closed he eyes tightly. The magic sparkles went away, but he was not a Prickle Pie Toad. He was still plain old Owen.

"Give it a try," Ella said and tickled Owen's nose.

Owen sneezed . . . but no fire came out!

"Hey! The spell worked!" a surprised Orlock said.

Owen gave his sister a look of relief.

Ella smiled and gave her brother a quick high five.

With Owen cured, the two dragons said their good-byes to Orlock the Evil (on Mondays and holidays only) Vegetable Wizard.

But the journey home wasn't as easy as the journey *to* the Cave of Aaaaah! Doom!

"We need to go left here," Owen said when they came to a fork in the path.

"No, we need to go right," Ella countered.

Every time Ella said "go left," Owen thought they should go right. If Owen said "up," then Ella said "down." If Ella said "backward," then Owen said "forward." If Owen said "peanut butter," then Ella said "jelly."

89

But the bickering got even worse when they spotted a tiny glowing winged girl no bigger than an ogre's toe.

"Look! It's the tree sprite we met earlier!" Owen waved to her. "Hi, there!" he called out.

"No, that's a water sprite for sure!" Ella replied.

"Tree sprite!"

"Water sprite!"

"Let's go ask!" they both said at the same time.

ZOOM!

They flew toward the sprite, who, seeing two dragons flying toward her shouting "tree sprite!" and "water sprite!" became scared and flew away.

The chase was on!

Just as they were about to grab the sprite, the two dragons crashed into each other.

BAM!

They tumbled down a hill through a patch of spider flowers and sticky slug weeds until . . .

SPLASH!

The twins fell into a cold lake of inky black water.

"This is all your fault!" they both yelled at each other at the same time.

But then Ella and Owen looked around
and realized something that was very not
good.

"Do you have any idea where we are?"
Owen asked.

"In a lake?" Ella replied.

"In a lake . . . and completely and totally
lost!" Owen replied.

"We're not lost!" Ella said. "Home is . . . that way! Or is it that way? Or . . ." Ella spun in circles, looking in every direction. She realized that they were indeed completely and totally lost. "I hate it when you're right. . . ." she said with a sigh.

And Owen was right. They were more
lost than a dwarf without a beard. . . .
Uh-oh!

Read on for a sneak peek from the second book in the Ella and Owen series, *Attack of the Stinky Fish Monster!*

BOOK 2
ELLA AND OWEN
ATTACK OF THE STINKY FISH MONSTER!
by Jaden Kent
illustrated by Iryna Bodnaruk

"**W**e are *not* lost!" Ella said to her twin brother as they swam through the water.

"Right," Owen said. He gave his sister a blank look. "We just fell down a big hill, splashed into this lake, and don't know our way home."

"You say that like it's a bad thing," Ella replied. "Don't worry. My dragon sense will lead the way."

"Dragon sense? Ha!" Owen laughed.

"My dragon sense led us to Osgood the ogre and also the Cave of Aaaaah! Doom! and the wizard Orlock Morlock, who cured your cold," Ella said proudly. "Just like I promised."

"You say that like it was a good thing!" Owen said. "Your dragon sense also got us into this mess and—whoa!" Owen flipped his tail out of the water. He looked behind himself nervously. "Something swam past me. Something BIG!"

"Don't be sil—*EEEEE!*" Ella screamed. "There *is* something in the water!" She began bobbing up and down.

"Maybe it's a friendly fish," Owen said hopefully. "A big friendly fish that wants to be friends because it's so friendly."

SPLASH! Suddenly, a huge Black Water Slime Eel jumped out from the water behind them. Its mouth snapped open. Giant fangs stuck out like tusks. Its angry scream sounded like an alarm. It was coming right at them.

"FLY AWAY!" Ella and Owen cried out at the same time.

Their dragon wings flapped as fast as wings can flap. They flew above the lake and—**BONK!** Ella and Owen crashed into each other.

SPLASH! They fell back into the water. The slime eel's back fin rose from the water like a sword. Its mouth opened, and it spit out the bones of a smaller fish. Huge fangs sparkled in the sun. Owen and Ella dove out of the way. The eel swam past, missing both of them.

"Grab the fin!" Ella yelled.

"No way!" Owen said. "That's crazy!"

Ella stretched her scaly arm and grabbed the slime eel's tail. "Follow me!"

"I'm too far away!" Owen yelled. "All I can grab is—" Owen grabbed Ella's tail.

The slime eel swam away fast, pulling Ella through the water. Owen hung on tightly.

"Stop tugging on my tail!" Ella yelled back to her brother.

"I'm trying to save you!" Owen shouted.

"That's so nice of you, but this is great! I'm a dragon cowgirl," Ella yelled. *"Yippee-ki-yay!"*

Then the slime eel lifted its tail out of the water and snapped it like a whip. Ella and Owen flew off the eel and headed toward the shore.

"AAAAAH!" they screamed as they sailed through the air.